Once Upon an Island

Once Upon an Island
Lila Linzer

PICTURES BY
Joan Luby

FRONT STREET
Asheville, North Carolina
1998

Library of Congress Cataloging-in-Publication Data

Linzer, Lila
Once Upon an Island / Lila Linzer; pictures by Joan Luby.
p. cm.
Summary: A collection of four fables which recount the adventures
of various animals living on the islands of the West Indies.
ISBN 1-886910-10-3 (alk. paper)
1. Fables, West Indies. 2. Tales – West Indies.
[1. Fables. 2. Folklore – West Indies]
I. Luby, Joan ill. II. Title.
PZ8.2.I470n 1998
398.2'09729 – dc21 98-12935

Once Upon an Island

Contents

I love telling stories. I love listening to them too. On the island where I live (just a little bit of a place in the middle of the Caribbean Sea) everyone seems to have a story. Sometimes if you're lucky she (or he) feels like sharing it.

On a just-so day, when it wasn't too hot and it wasn't too cool, Tanty Pearl told me one of hers. We were standing right there in the middle of her kitchen.

With the Magnificent Conch it was a different thing altogether. He was out in the fields, looking over his pigs and goats ... that's where he remembered a story he heard when he was a boy.

And once when Vincent came to visit, he told me a story his granny used to tell him and his sisters when it was time to go to bed and they didn't want to.

Yes, they all told me stories just the way they tell them in the West Indies. And I remember them just that way. Now I'd like to take you there, to that very special faraway place where strange and wonderful things happen ... sometimes. Where cows may forget their friends and lizards know more than you think ... where grasshoppers laugh and spiders talk to dragon-flies. They all talk, you see. And the way they sound is the way things are ... on my island.

Lila Linzer
St Croix

Special Friends

"You don't know what gon'
happen till it happen!"

Long ago, on a faraway island, at that secret-secret place where the ocean meet the sky, on an early mornin of a pretty-pretty day, nothin specially *unusual* was happenin. But me darlin, on that very day, when the sun was shinin bright like it always shine, an' the breeze was blowin easy like it always blow, an' the sky was lookin fine like it always look, an' the birds was singin sweet like they always sing…well on that particular day, something unusual was a-*bout* to happen.

It all start under the spreadin-out branches of a big ol sea-grape. Cow was feelin sleepy, as usual. An' Egret was busy chattin away, as usual.

"Momma Cow," she call. "Look here, the mornin light so clear-clear."

Cow raise up her ears at *that*. Yeah, Egret always

callin her Momma Cow, just 'cause she does enjoy it so!

"Mmm, mm," Egret chatter. "This breeze feelin so gentle today. I glad indeed we did rise up so early this mornin."

Cow give a contented rumble, down there in her stomach, the way cows do sometimes.

"Egret," she say. "I does have a little itch, straight back a me neck...there."

An' Egret just pick that itch clean away. Cow an' Egret do most everything together. It please them to do it that way.

Well. It a truly fine day all right. But not for Ol Brother Bee.

"Who it is I can worry now?" that ol troublemaker wonder.

An' when he spy Cow an' Egret chattin so happy together...why, buzz-buzz-buzz...he go directly over to Cow's ear. "You payin attention, ol friend? 'Cause I got something important to tell."

Now that sly Ol Brother Bee, he flyin up an' back, up an' back, front a Cow's face.

"What for you need Egret, eh?" he buzz. "It *you* do all the labor, carryin her round on your broad, hardworkin back. She havin a merry time, all right...an' up to now she never even get her feathers ruffle."

So. Cow chewin her cud just like always.

"He sensible in truth," she grumble. "What I need that lazy Egret for any-ol-way?"

An' she raise up her head. An' she bellow, "I finish doin all the work round here. It *me* does the walkin, *me* does the climbin, *me* does the huntin. An' what you do, Miss Lazy-Do-Nothin? You come 'long for the ride, eh? Well, carryin finish, time done."

Then it was that Cow give herself a mighty shake. An' oh my! Wasn't that little bird real startle!

"What all this confusion?" she screech. "You makin joke, Momma Cow? Don't I keep you clean clean clean? Don't I love you true true true?"

An' Egret lookin in Cow's eyes all the while. But Cow not listenin. No sir! She just keep shakin her head, side to side. So poor little Egret…at last she give up an' fly away.

Well. *You* don't know an' *I* don't know why Cow done any listenin to Ol Brother Bee. But she done it. An' that a fact.

Now you might suppose Cow gon' miss Egret right away. But she don't. She too busy feelin important 'bout the whole thing. An' by-'n-by them pesty little bugs, them itchy-itchy ones…they come straight back to Cow's brown coat again. An' in the evenin' when the sun was

gettin ready to set an' the sky was gettin ready to darken
…well, Cow would kneel down under her old sea-grape…
an' she would be feelin lonely.

"Oh me, oh my," Cow groanin. "Brother Bee go an'
mess-up the whole thing. He always be interferin. An' me
not ponderin one little bit…just playin bold an' brave,
bold an' brave. Now here I be…one foolish, rude, down-
hearted cow, in truth!"

Then it was that she did raise up her head an' bawl,
"Egret, Egret, me dear sweet friend. Where you be now?"

But, me darlin, it too late for that. Egret couldn't hear
Cow callin. Not at-all. After that hurtful quarrel, well…
Egret was feelin so sad. You not gon' catch her lingerin
long where she not wanted.

Now Momma Cow *big* you know. An' she slow-movin.
But she determine! She gon' find Egret. So she set out
huntin.

"Blue Mountain be a place where Egret does love to
find a shady rest," Cow mumble. "Maybe I try there, first
thing." So she walk, walk, walk…right into that rainy
rain-forest.

Ah, but she sure not noticin them flowers bloomin
in the cracks a rocks. An' she not even listenin to the
tree frogs whistlin in the dusky-dusky shade. No! All she
longin for was to find Egret.

But Egret not there, me darlin. No! An' she not down in Cotton Valley…not over by Spring Garden…not out to Grassy Point…uh-*uh*. An' when Cow done finish climbin *way* up top a Figtree Hill…well, Egret not there neither.

"What I gon' call *this*?" Cow wonder.

An' she start to feel weary, in truth. She search so hard, it seem like she done search the whole a the island. An' everywhere she go, she askin, "Maybe *you* did see Egret? I missin her so."

But Cow not gettin no answers. Not a one!

Oh, me darlin, that day was hot. So hot Cow's skin make a glisten in the noonday sun.

"Mmm, I be lookin an' lookin," Cow mumble to herself. "When it be I gon' do some findin? There got to be *some*body did see Egret *some*time. Where everybody be these days?"

But all them animals she meet…you *know* they not wantin to help Cow nohow. 'Cause she did hurt sweet Egret for no reason at-all.

So when Cow come walkin up to Browny Pelican an' Missy Yellowbird an' Cousin Goat, an' all them others… well, they just run off or jump down or look away or get real busy. All 'cept Mister Mongoose.

When he hear Cow callin, "Hey-hey," there outside

his hole, Mister Mongoose pick up his head an' mumble, "Egret gone off? Shame-shame on you, Momma Cow." An' with a twitch a his flat-flat tail, he slip back down. An' there Cow standin, lookin at nothin at-all.

Ah me, Cow was gettin discouraged. Yes indeed. But she not no giver-upper neither.

"Well. This be a riddle without no answer," she mutter. "I know Egret always be chattin. If someone don't *see* her, they got to *hear* her." An' then it was that Cow did stumble over a stickin-up piece a coral-stone. An' wouldn't you know...all stretch out, just takin the sun, be none other than Wise Ol Lizard.

"'Scuse me for disturbin you nappin, Mister Lizard, but I been huntin Egret all over the place. I hope in me heart may be it *you* did see her."

Lizard slowly open his big-big eyes. His tongue come out his mouth, an' then it go back in. His body arch right up, an' then it go back down. His tail curl round this way, an' then it curl round that way.

An' just when Cow thinkin Lizard asleep for true, he go an' pick up his scaly-scaly head. An' he look straight at Cow. An' he say, "Why you treat your good friend so bad she turn an' leave you, eh? I sure I don't know where she be now. Sorry. Sorry." An' he close his big sleepy eyes tight shut again.

Well. After that, Cow real ashame. She feelin so low, she can't think where to go.

"Egret gone, in truth," she sigh. "Water come to me eyes whenever I think a her. Even the trees them actin sad," she say. So not sayin even one more word, Cow go an' kneel right down, down under that prickly ol calabash tree. She was *that* despairin!

Now, me darlin, sometimes when you feelin real sad, you can't keep lookin down. That the time for lookin up. An' that exactly what Cow did do. She raise up her head to see where she be an'...sittin up there on top the tree was Egret herself, lookin so sweet.

How it was them two did reach the self-same tree at the self-same time, eh? Now that be a puzzle, for certain.

"How-do, Egret?" Cow mumble so quiet you couldn't hardly hear her.

"How's yourself, Momma Cow?" that little white bird did answer.

"You been hidin here all this time?" Cow call. But Egret makin no reply at-all. Now *you* know an' *I* know how loud-loud Egret could screech, if only she be wantin to. But here she was, stayin quiet...just smoothin her feathers an' lookin down at Momma Cow.

A course, Cow must a knowed Egret's feelins was hurt serious. An' now this gettin back together again not goin easy at-all.

"I real sorry," Cow mumble in a low-low voice.

"What's that, Momma Cow?" Egret call. "I don't hear you so good."

"What for you restin up there, Egret?" Cow shout out. "Don't you know I feelin sorry, in truth?" An' then her voice get softer still. "Don't you know it gon' take me three hundred years to get the shame out me heart? Don't you know I askin you to…come back, an'…be best friends …like always?"

Oh my! That little bird did start to twinkle like the brightest star. 'Cause *you* know an' *I* know how true she does love Cow. So it don't take but a minute before she fly straight down…

"Right back home on your strong brown back, Momma Cow," she whisper. "Just like I never been gone at-all."

Well. Them two friends did talk talk talk. They was chattin when the sun drop down. An' they was chattin still when the moon rise up. Egret say, "Ooh, ooh, it almost time for mornin light to come, an' yet me eyes wide open so. Please, Momma Cow. Remember me one a your heart-to-hearts. Nothin in the world sweeter than that."

So. The two a them did settle theyselves, right there an' then. An' Cow…she start out in the softest, the sweet-

MOMMA COW'S SONG

West Indian rhythm (lively)

by Lila Linzer

When the sun shine yel —— low yellow
(When the moon hang hea —— vy heavy)

An' the day start fine an' new,
(An' the sky turn dark an' blue,)

An' the bree —— zes ti —— ckle tickle,
(An' the night sounds whi —— sper whisper,)

Mom-ma Cow is lo—vin' you

Oo ———————————————— Your

Mom —ma Cow lovin' you ———— !

Oo ———————————————— Your

Mom —ma Cow lovin' you! ———— !

est, the gentlest now-it-time-to-sleep-way she know.

"Hush now, Egret," Cow talkin low. "I gon' tell you a real true heart-to-heart."

When the sun shine yellow-yellow,
An' the day start fine an' new,
An' the breezes tickle-tickle,
Momma Cow is lovin you.

When the moon hang heavy-heavy,
An' the sky turn dark an' blue,
An' the night sounds whisper-whisper,
Momma Cow is lovin you.

An' so the night did pass, an' the day did come.

The breeze was as soft as a baby lamb's nose, an' the air was as cool as a fresh sea cucumber, an' the sun was risin up an' scatterin shadows wherever he go, an' the little land-creatures all hustlin an' bustlin to get the day goin'.

Well, just like always, soon as she open up her eyes, Egret start in to chat. "Momma Cow," she say. "Stir yourself, darlin. I got somethin important to tell you. Late in the night, when the moon was goin' down...down into the sea...just when I was fixin to fall asleep...this idea come into me head. Let we have the biggest, the bestest, the grandest bush party in hist'ry…"

Cow pick up her head. "In hist'ry?" she laugh. She was that happy.

Egret twitter, "Let we have kalalu an' papalu an' long-top an' tan-tan an' mango an' sour-sop an' —"

"Egret," Cow say sternly. "You chatterin like a magpie an' jumpin higher than a mountain chicken."

Egret stop still an' look down. But Cow not serious, don't you know. Her eye have a twinkle in it.

"Go on, go on," Cow chuckle. "I likes when you do like that."

Well, me darlin, that's exactly what they gone an' done. Yes sir, they had the biggest gatherin' of animals the island ever see. An' up to now, I never did hear a no other! Oh my, ain't Cow an' Egret work hard, searchin out a special somethin for each an' every*one* a their friends. Yeah, that's them two all right … all-time thinkin an' carin, thinkin an' carin.

At last the big day come, with the weather just so.

"Look, Momma Cow," Egret call. "Look them animals comin now, all in a procession. An' the littlest one comin first, as usual."

Well, Egret start gettin busy then … meetin an' greetin an' makin them feel all comfortable.

"Good day, good day," she sing out to Yellowbird an'

Grey Dove, Pelican an' Billy Goat. "Sweet hibiscus here for you, Missy…crispy tan-tan seeds waitin, Aunty…look these slippy silverfish, Uncle…come have a taste a *this*, Cousin."

Uh-*huh!* Egret keepin busy all right, when Mongoose come an' peep his head from back a gumberry tree.

"Come along, come along," Egret encouragin him. "I know you be the most bashful animal on the island. But look at all the others them…havin fun an' eatin good. This party nice like anything." Egret smile. An' she fluff up her feathers with wonder an' delight.

"See there how he creepin in," she show Momma Cow. Egret sure proud a *that*.

Well, things goin great when all of a sudden Cow see something movin in the bush.

"Look. Look yonder, Egret. It Ol Brother Bee himself. What that scamp doin, hangin round here anyway?"

But Egret so happy, she wantin *every*one be happy. "Ah, come on Momma Cow," Egret whisper. "We glad. We *so* glad. Let we ask him, too."

An' *that* how come Brother Bee slip in with all the rest.

A course, me darlin, there couldn't be no party without Lizard. An' he be the *slowest*, the *pokiest*, the *laziest* lizard you ever did see. But he get there. Just in time.

"Come right along, Mister Lizard," Egret call out. "This sunny rock be the kind a warm spot you always does enjoy. We did set it here 'cause we knowed you comin."

Well, Cow look at Lizard. An' Lizard look at Cow. They rememberin. Hmm. It Lizard make Cow feel so ashame when she huntin for Egret. An' now here Lizard sayin, "These be the good times, eh?" Then Cow know things all right, for real.

Oh my, what a spree they had. An' after all that eatin an' all that dancin … so much dancin in fact, that the ground did tremble an' the leaves did shake …well, after all a that, Cow an' Egret be just sort a strollin round, checkin on things, when sudden-like, the clearin get kind a quiet.

"There," Egret say. "See all them animals, Momma Cow? They done eat an' eat an' dance an' dance till they can't move no more. Look here, they all fixin to go straight off to sleep. I do believe this gon' be the sleepiest bush-party in hist'ry."

But Cow don't mind it one bit, no sir! The sun high, the sky blue, an' Egret…"she back for keeps," Cow thinkin. An' she smile. "Come on an' settle down, ol friend," Cow whisper. "With the trees them rustlin, an' the sun so shiny-shiny, we gon' take us a little nap. The heat a the day be the very best time for nappin, don't you know."

So that *just* what they went an' did.

Well me darlin, we comin to the end a this real true tale ... since from that day to this, Cow an' Egret never had no other quarrel. An' if you ever *do* go out in the countryside ... out where the pastures be ... Well, that where you gon' find them ... Big Brown Cow an Little White Egret, always together. 'Cause they *know* something. An' now you know it too.

Poor Mornin Dove

"Mango sweet, lemon tart —
story sad, break your heart."

When daylight come, me darlin, it amazin how things break up. Secret night start makin shivers. An' the sky gettin lighter-lighter. All the hills them black...then turn to gray...then turn to green. An' the sun-red get all mix up with the sea-blue. Ah yes, me dear, every day does have a daybreak...an' it on one a them cool, clear, shimmer-shimmer, everyday-daybreaks that Missy Mongoose up so early. She out huntin her breakfast an' who she does meet but Mornin Dove herself.

"Good day, good day," Missy say. "My, you lookin busy this mornin, sweetheart. What it is you doin?" Missy always bein sociable, you know.

"How come it just *now* you gettin interested, huh?" Mornin Dove answer. "I doin what I doin since always. Startin up the day, that what I doin." An' she keep on goin'.

"Just wonderin, that all," Missy mumble. An' she slip away quick-quick.

Well, Mornin Dove not gon' bother with all that wonderin, no, no. She have a whole day's work to do. An' no whole day to do it in neither.

Well, I got to tell you, me darlin. Mornin Dove didn't always talk so rush-an'-fuss, no sir! You should a seen how it was in the Days Before. Things different then. An' Mornin Dove…well, she on top a the world.

A course you know she been a gray bird for always, right? But in them days her feathers a pearly gray. A light-light soft-*soft* pearly gray. Mmm, it make you feel good just lookin at her! An' the song she sing…her voice so sweet an' clear, the minute you hear it, your mood gon' change for the better.

Mornin's the time
When the sun come to play.
He say to me,
"Come an' start up the day."
You gon' to love
All the things what I do.
Gettin the world
Shiny-bright an' all new.

32

MORNIN DOVE SONG

West Indian rhythm (lively)

by Lila Linzer

Mornin's the time when the Sun come to play

He say to me 'come an' start up the day

You gon' to love all the things what I do

Gettin' the World shiny bright an' all new. Sing

out ____! Chase them shadows a-way. Sing

out ____! It a sweet new bran' day. Sing

out ____! Can you see the sky-blue? Sing

out ! Glad I do it for you ____!

Sing OUT!
Chase them shadows away.
Sing OUT!
It a sweet new-bran' day.
Sing OUT!
Can't you see the sky-blue?
Sing OUT!
Glad I do it for you.

Yes indeed. Back in the ol days, when all this start-up stuff get goin, Mornin Dove a one-an'-only, for true. Oh my, yes! She happy an' singin wherever she go. Spreadin joy an' doin good. That be Mornin Dove, in the ol days.

See, back then be a special, in-between time. It hers, all hers. Before Day come, when it not dark an' it not light, an' things still-still, an' nothin happenin. Well, there be Mornin Dove, with her black-black eyes them pop right open.

"It time," she say to herself. (Mornin Dove all-time talkin to herself.) "It time." An' she shake she feathers. An' she stretch she wings. An' she get goin'.

Now how she know when to get started, eh? *That* a good question! Could be it a mornin star did *sing* her up. Could be it a gentlin breeze did *tickle* her up. Could be. But she know when to get up, all right. An' she do it.

So…it one a them ol-time mornins. An' Li'l Cricket an' he momma just fixin to go off to sleep. They peepin out from 'tween some lemon grass. An' they see Mornin Dove. She flyin up, *way*-way up. An' she takin the tip end of a great big leave-over-from-the-night cloud. An' she dip in she sharp-sharp beak, an' she pull…an' she pull. An' before you know what goin on, that cloud gone. She done roll it up-up from in front a Sun's face, and guess what? Day come!

"How she do that, Momma?" Li'l Cricket askin.

"Magic," he momma tell him.

"What magic be, Momma?" Li'l Cricket askin.

"Magic when somethin' happen an' you don't know how. That's magic," he momma tell him. An' then she ease him off to sleep. 'Cause believe it or not, crickets does sleep in the day!

Well. Mornin Dove got plenty more to do, don't you know. Seem like she here, she there, she every-which-where. That bird a four-star worker, in truth. Chile, she *workin!* She got to polish them sunbeams, make 'em shiny-shiny. And she got to sweep up them spiderwebs in all them hide-aways, make the place clean-clean. An' she got to chase them shadows, even the teeniest-tiniest hard-to-see-but-they-there shadows. Oh yes, she got to do all that. An' she got to do more, too. She got to shake off the dewdrops, every last one, get the leaves them, dry-dry an' ready for the day. She do it, all right. An' she do it every self-same day.

"I *got* to do it," Mornin Dove say to herself. "Else how day gon' happen, if I don't?"

So things goin' along in they good ol ways, when for no reason I never hear tell, Mornin Dove begin to change. Just a little at first. But she start forgettin some a her nice-nice ways.

She forget to say "If you please" when she ask Yellowbird to dig up some worms, extra for her.

"I got no time for worm-huntin'," she say. "Carry me some a them tomorrow."

That the way Mornin Dove say it. An' *that* not too nice, eh?

An' next mornin, when Yellowbird come over with some them fat-fat juicy ones, extra for her, well, she forget to say, "thanks darlin," when she should a.

An' she forget to say "'Scuse me Honey" when she brush away Honey Bee's nest by accident.

An' she forget to say "How-do" an' "Good day" an' such. Yeah, she forgettin lots a things.

Well. The animals them start gettin vex with her. They not likin it one little bit.

"Things not bein like they use to be," Snail

complainin.

"Where our ol sweet Mornin Dove anyway?" Yellowbird thinkin.

"Why she gone an' change so?" Missy wonderin.

But Spider, he madder than mad. "Hey! This goin' too far, in truth," he sputter. "Who Mornin Dove think she be, anyhow?"

Dragonfly not answerin. He just listenin, but he look like he agreein.

Okay, so then Spider start tellin him, "That Mornin Dove, she gettin too big, for true. She so prideful... she rude... she think she better than anything."

"Well what it is you want, huh?" Dragonfly ask Spider. "What it *is?*"

"I want her stop breakin up me webs. That's what," Spider answer back. "I spin hard-hard all the night, eh? An' in the mornin, me webs them all mash-up. What kind a business you call *that?*" An' he eyes flashin an' he legs goin like crazy.

"You right, Brother, you right," Snail chime in. He nearby, restin out a the hot sun. "I hear what you sayin."

Well, Spider surprise at *that.* He never been too friendly with Snail beforetimes. But now it look like they gettin together. Okay. So Spider get back to the problem.

"How we gon' stop Mornin Dove from cleanin up the

whole place?" he say. "Since she think up this I-start-the-day-thing she get so boastful, it just ridiculous."

"Yeah, yeah," Yellowbird nod her head. "She never give me the time a day no more. She think she too high an' mighty for that."

Well, here when the sun start slippin down-down an' the shadows start growin long-long. Soon the night creatures creepin out from every-which-where. See, it the *shadows* them need for hidin. An' the evenin cool makin it comfortable all over the place. Yeah. Night-time be the right time for them to do they things.

"The darker the better," Bat always sayin. Anyway, they comin out, left an' right, an' they gettin busy. Crab pop her head out a her sandy hole an' she ask, "What happenin, what happenin?"

Centipede come wigglin along, an' he keep right on goin'. He don't say nothin, but he listenin hard.

An' all the while it gettin darker an' darker.

"Look, look there. Night comin down," Momma Cricket show her little one. "The stars them findin they ways back into they self-same places."

"How they do that, Momma?" Li'l Cricket ask.

"Magic," he momma tell him.

Now Li'l Cricket know what magic *be*, he don't need to ask no more. So they join right in with all them others. An' pretty soon you got Tree Frog, you got Crab, you got Snail, you got Li'l Cricket an' he momma, you got Bat, you got Night Bird, you got Lightenin Bug. You *even* got Dragonfly. He don't stay out nights, usual. But he so interested in what happenin, he forget his sleepin time.

"Remember the days when Mornin Dove sweeter than sugar?" Yellowbird askin. (She stayin up late too.)

"I not talkin 'bout what *was*," Spider snap back. "I talkin 'bout what is."

Now he gettin hot all right.

"Have to be somethin can change it round." That what Spider tell 'em.

Well, me darlin, they all start buzzin then. An' before you know it, somebody come up with a plan.

"We need a night without no end. That what we need." It *Crab* come up with it. Sometime Crab do get a good idea. Sometime.

"No more hot sun to dry me skin," Tree Frog whistlin.

"Plenty shadows to hide me trail," Snail laughin.

"All we got to do is get Mornin Dove to quit that I-start-the-day stuff, an' things gon' be fine an' dandy," Bat say. He gettin in the swing of it now, an' he goin' along with all them others.

Now you know lizards be night creatures too, but Wise Ol Lizard *not* joinin in. No sir! He off by himself where nobody see him, an' he hearin it all.

"What a bunch a foolishness," he chuckle. "Sun don't need no help. He gon' rise, no matter what." Lizard know

plenty, but he not tellin.

"Look here. This what we gon' do." Night Bird chirpin an' flittin from place to place. "Know that sticky-bush where Mornin Dove does like to sleep? Well, when she settle down for her night-time rest, *that* when we gon' do it. We gon' get some sleepy-dust out a Red Hibiscus, an' we gon' sprinkle it on Mornin Dove to keep her sleepin good. An' then, then…it all depend on Spider. He got to spin a web all round Mornin Dove. It got to be strong. It got to hold her so she can't do none them early-mornin things she all-time doin."

Well! The animals them lookin at Spider next. It all depend on him. Oh boy, Spider feelin big like anything now. He feelin like a natural-born leader, in truth.

"When this gon' happen, Spider? When this gon' happen?" Tree Frog real excited.

"This number-one plan goin down *tomorrow night!*" Spider announce. He proud a heself now.

"What Mornin Dove gon' say, Momma?" Li'l Cricket chirpin quiet-quiet.

"Hush up, honey," he momma say. "This a time for listenin." An' he hush up.

All the other animals them wonderin then.

"Maybe that too-too soon."

"How 'bout we think things over first."

"This gon' be big-big for sure."

Yeah. Some a the animals them wonderin, all right … but it too late for that. When things rollin, they rollin.

So. The next night, when it *that* dark even the moon havin trouble findin a place to shine, they all there. Every-which-one a them. They startin out together, in full force. An' it Lightenin Bug does show 'em the way. He flashin his light an' he lookin important. So … they on they way to Mornin Dove's sleepin place … an' they walkin … but they not talkin, no sir! This *serious*, an' they know it.

"Can't wake her now. Gon' mess up the whole thing," Dragonfly whisper.

He not tellin secrets, me darlin. It just that dragonflies does whisper, that's all.

An' a course, when they reach over to Grassy Point, she there … sleepin like she always sleep. She all curl up in a small-small ball a gray feathers. You can't even see her head at-all when she sleepin.

"But we not gon' *hurt* Mornin Dove?" Yellowbird askin quiet. She startin to feel real bad now.

"No, no. That definite!" Spider answer. "What you think … we wicked or somethin?"

"We just gon' keep her still till Night come down good-good," Night Bird add in.

See, some a the animals worryin if this be the right thing. Yeah, they thinkin 'bout that. But Spider, he keepin things movin … an' Night Bird all ready … an' everyone a them want night to last long-long. So they all go along with it … that the way things happen sometimes … folks goin' along with it.

Now Lizard be there too, off a ways in the bush. He standin by an' he seein the whole thing through.

"What gon' be, gon' be," he thinkin. "I *knows* what I *knows*." An' he settle down quiet.

So … here where the action get started. Night Bird been carryin some a that whispery, fine-like-powder sleepy-dust Red Hibiscus always hidin. An' he takin his time, 'cause he want do this thing right. He carry it watchful, an' he sprinkle it gentle. An' it settle down all over Mornin Dove softer-than-soft. An' Mornin Dove … well, she just keep on sleepin, better than ever.

Now it time for Spider to do his thing. An' he ready … an' he willin … an' he all set to do what he got to do. Spider workin so careful-careful, his eyes squeeze up tight. He start spinnin … but he not spinnin no see-through, fly-away, lacy-tracy, slippy-slidy web, uh-*uh!* He spinnin for real now, an' he know his web got to hold her there, tight, till night come down an' stay for always. No one hear him when he workin. No one *ever* hear Spider when

he workin, but he workin...hard! An' just in time, too.
'Cause the sky startin to change, gettin sort a light. An'
the animals them gettin restless.

"This me regular time for sleepin," Bat rustle he wings.
"Maybe I better be headin back."

"No, no. Wait up. Things gon' turn out good. You
see," Crab tell him. So he wait.

Well, Spider keep on spinnin, but Mornin Dove start
to stir...just a bit. She open she eyes, an' when she find
she can't even move a feather, she shriek out, "What
this *be*?"

Oh my, Mornin Dove distress, all right. "I got to do
me things," she callin. "It 'most time for Sun to rise. How
he gon' do that without I helpin him?"

An' she start to wiggle an' pull an' push an' twist. She
tryin to get out, an' that web holdin her. Spider done it
good, all right. So things holdin. So far.

Now it was that this funny thing did happen. Ol' Sun,
he peep up he head, way-way out by that sea-water-
sky-water place. You know the
place, it so far-far you can't
see if it water or what. Well.
He peep up an' he keep on
comin. He risin, all right...
an' he doin it by heself.

"How this happenin?" Crab want to know.

"This not part a the plan," Bat grumblin.

"I travel far an' see a lot," Night Bird gettin upset, "but I never see nothin like this."

Well, me darlin, them animals in a state of confusion! All that plannin, all that doin, an' now they come to see there nothin in it at-all. (Things does turn out like that sometimes.)

"I guess Night *Night* an' Day *Day* an' that *that*." Centipede say. An' he keep on goin.

"You right, Brother, you right," Snail pipe up.

Maybe Snail a slow crawler, but he a fast thinker, all right. An' he know what's what.

So. The night creatures them all start to slip away. See, Mornin Dove loose herself by now. Her feathers all rumple an' everything. But she loose. An' the animals lookin ashame, all right. So they not stayin.

Oh my, an' there be Mornin Dove, alone-alone an' feelin *so* sad. Her feathers them what all-time use to be so soft an' pearly…yeah, *them* feathers…seem like they gettin all drab-down…sort a dull-like. An' the shimmer…it all gone. Her two eyes open big-big. An' she just sit there, watchin Sun rise up all on his own. It hard to believe, eh? Well, me darlin, that when she start in to cry. It a strange thing all right, hearin Mornin Dove cry. She just learnin how to do it, but she not ever gon' forget it. 'Cause you see, from that day to this, Mornin Dove never sing again.

Darlin, remember how it was…when she did sing in the ol days?

You gon' to love
All the things what I do.
Gettin the world
Shiny-bright an' all new.

An' now…never again! No, it *cryin* she do for ever-more. An' when you out in the countryside, an' you up early-early, you gon' hear Mornin Dove, all right. An' you gon' hear her cryin for the ol ways…them times when only *she* could make Day come. She learn a lesson, yes she learn it. But it too late now. 'Cause it like the ol folks always say, "When you got a good thing goin', better keep it goin'."

Monkey Come – Monkey Go

"When words a wisdom comin down,
better ask ...who talkin?"

"Things never simple, no sir," Goat grumble. "One minute you think you know what goin' on, next minute…"

"What you talkin 'bout, Red-Eye?" Lizard push right in. "You always talkin-talkin an' sayin nothin."

Goat turn right round an' look Lizard straight in the face. "You know I vex when you call me Red-Eye."

"What you want me call you, when you the only goat I know what have red eyes?" Lizard answer back.

"Me eyes them red with no sleepin. That why they red. I all-time thinkin 'bout things. An' up to now I got no answer, neither."

"Well, what the question, eh? What the question?" ask Lizard. He got more patience than most, it true. But when he start to lose it, he lose it.

"Look, we got a monkey-no-climb tree, an' we got a

monkey-puzzle bush, right? So how come I never seen no monkey on this island, never?" Now Goat gettin' real excited too.

"Okay, okay." Lizard nod he head. "I gon' tell you how that happen. But remember. No eatin while I story-tellin. An' no scramblin round neither. It break me concentration."

So then an' there they settle down. An' Lizard start he tellin.

No one know how it be that Monkey come to here. It a mystery, for sure. Some say he must a come from Yonder. Some say it must a been from Back Beyond. Who know? But it happen, all right. Over by Grapetree Beach. That where it happen.

Oh, it just a regular, everyday, nothin-special kind a mornin back then when Monkey come sailin in. He jump off the big bamboo he travelin on. An' he land directly on that crispy sand you does find down there.

"Mm, mmm," Monkey say. "This weather feelin mighty fine. The sky my kind a blue. An' them mountains so high-high, they look like they liftin theyself up-up-up. Uh-*huh*! Clouds always be hangin round them type a mountains. That's a fact. An' when cloud call, rain fall. Banana love rain. Monkey love banana. I stayin."

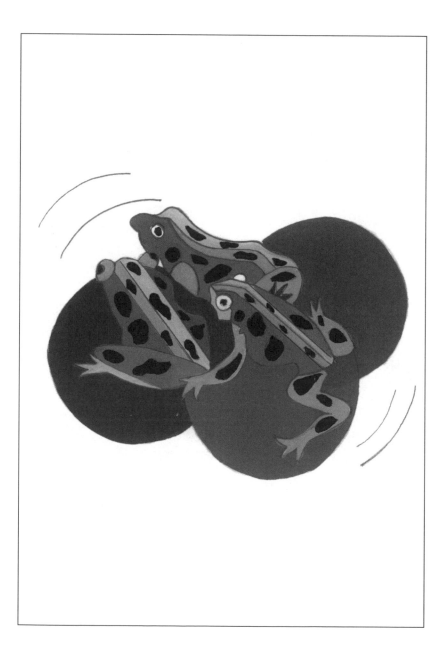

An' quicker-than-quick he off, makin he way through the bush.

"Hey, Uncle, this here story gettin good," Goat shout out.

"What I tell you, Red-Eye?" Lizard start fussin. "If you mouth open, me mouth shut."

So Goat quiet heself down fast-fast.

Well meantime, way-way over to West End, near where Dry River does empty out, the frogs them be havin they troubles, all right. They havin troubles in doubles.

"Hold it, Uncle, hold it," Goat bawl out. "What frogs you talkin 'bout?"

"What frogs?" Lizard snap back. "The frogs what live over there. *Them* frogs! Now listen, Red-Eye. One more time you mix me up, an' I gone."

"Okay, okay. Keep you skin on." Goat all-time askin questions. He just that curious.

See, what you have here be a problem story. An' it the frogs what *be* the problem. All them different kind a frogs! You got the bull frogs an' the tree frogs an' the pond frogs an' the bush frogs. You got the tree frogs whistlin when the bull frogs sleepin, an' the jumpers jumpin when the grunters eatin! You got commotion, confusion, confliction an' distraction. Pandemonium be the word a the day!

Well, with all that rantin an' ravin an' clashin an' mashin, I mean, it just ridiculous how they quarrelin. It look like no way they gon' get theyself together. Believe me, things goin' from bad to worse.

Well now, a time come when all that racket they makin 'most reach down to East End. One a the frogs them jump up top a rock an' call out loud-loud.

"Hey! Hey!" Blinky shoutin. (That he name, Blinky.) An' all the frogs them stop right then.

"What goin' on round here a disgrace, in truth. It need changin fast," he say.

Well, the frogs them start mumblin.

"What he want?"

"How we gon' change things?"

"Who he, anyway?"

An' such.

"What we need," Blinky shoutin for real now, "be a Settler."

Now *that* got the frogs listenin hard all right.

"A Settler? What that?" Bull Frog ask.

"Well," Blinky answer, "a Settler tell you what to do,

who be wrong, who be right, who got to go, who get to stay. A Settler know how to settle things. That a Settler." An' Blinky sit down.

Well. All the frogs them start lookin round then. The tree frogs givin whispers to each other like crazy.

"What he mean?"

"What he say?"

"What you think?"

An' such.

Bull Frog stand up on top the rock next, puff out he big-big cheeks, an' croak, "Sound good to me. How we gon' find this Settler? That the big question now!" An' he sit down too.

Well you know there be one frog never hold still at-all at-all, an' that frog be Pinky. He jump, he screech, he sing, he bounce. You all-time know when Pinky near by. An' here come Pinky, jumpin to beat the band.

"I know, I know," he squeal. "The ol-time, big-big, strong-strong, never-move, seen-it-all banyan tree heself. We gon' make Ol' Banyan our Settler. An' we gon' call him King. A tree got to like that, for sure."

So that how the frogs choose them a Settler. That tree *big*. It real big. It don't move. It don't shake. It just stand there. It root reach down-to-down. An' it branch stretch up-to-up. It *old*. It *very* old. It been here so long, it know every thing there is. Yes sir, the frogs choose them a Settler. An' they did call him King.

Then Lizard look over at Goat to see if he payin attention. An' he was.

Well, a feelin a pure joy did spread all over them frogs. It make me feel good just rememberin it.

Then Long-Toe cheer out, "Hooray! We got something goin' here, all right. Who could ever a believe it?"

An' now things start gettin busy. 'Cause if there be one thing frogs know, it how to get busy.

"Who bringin Ol Banyan somethin' pretty-pretty?" Chook-Chook call out. "Somethin' what gon' get him in the mood. That what we need!"

"What you thinkin of, Chook-Chook? Some flower maybe?" Lala ask him.

"Maybe," Chook-Chook agree.

So quicker-than-quick, the frogs them out there, gatherin flowers like there no tomorrow. They carryin lemon drop an' periwinkle, lilac tree an' frangipani, cup-a-gold an' red hibiscus, daisy-free, an' lazy-mazy. Pretty soon it lookin like a rainbow come to rest on Ol Banyan foot.

"Give a look those flowers them. They smellin sweet

all right," Lala smile.

"True is true," Long-Toe always bein agreeable. "Colors sure does lift things up."

"Yeah, yeah." Buffo mutter. "But Ol Banyan, he keepin awful quiet."

"How he gon' know he a Settler now?" Grichi wonderin.

"Maybe we got to *tell* him," Pinky squeal out.

"Okay," Bull Frog croak. "You tell him."

"Uh-*uh*. Not me." Pinky turn all bashful now.

"Okay, okay. I do it." Chook-Chook step up. "Mister Banyan, sir," he whisper. "You a Settler now," an' he sit down real quick.

"How he gon' hear that?" the frogs them sayin.

"You voice so soft-soft."

"Raise it up, Chook, raise it up."

"He not never gon' hear that."

An' such.

Poor Chook-Chook embarrass, all right. "Huh," he grunt. "*You* bigger than me, Buffo. You do it."

Well, well, well. Here they go again, throwin them cross words round in they bad ol ways. Oh yes, them frogs gettin into it for real now.

"Wait a minute, wait a minute," Chook-Chook yellin. "We got to get organize, we got to get organize."

"You right, you right." Grichi goin' 'long with the whole thing. "We holdin a meetin, but we not gettin anywhere."

"Ol Banyan ain't talkin. He ain't even rustlin," Blinky chime in. "Uh-*uh*, things not lookin too good, eh?"

"Well," Bull Frog croak. "Could be Ol Banyan don't want to be a Settler. Could be we got to talk him into it."

Well Red-Eye, the frogs them start gettin restless.

They jumpin an' hoppin, squealin an' puffin. Look like the earth-self be movin.

"Hey, hey, Uncle," Goat break in. "Where Monkey now?"

"What you askin, Red-Eye? Who tellin this story anyhow?" Lizard say. "Don't worry yourself 'bout Monkey, 'cause Monkey comin any time now." Then Lizard raise up he head so he lookin straight at Goat. "What I tell you 'bout talkin when I talkin?"

"Okay, okay. Take it easy," Goat say an' he settle down good-good.

See, Monkey out in the bush there. But he comin closer-closer. He see all them frogs but he don't know what they doin. And he don't care, neither. He tired out, all right, an' he need a lie-down.

"The more I walkin, the more far them mountains

be," Monkey say to heself. "Walkin done for this day. An' that's *that*."

So he start lookin for a good take-it-easy place.

Well, that when he notice Ol Banyan.

"Look, look a there." Monkey real please with it. "That a mighty comfortable-lookin tree, all right. It gon' suit me perfect."

A course Monkey know how to climb a tree from the top. So he not worry 'bout all them frogs down at the bottom. All he got to do is slip up that neighbour-tree there, an' when the frogs not lookin, why he swing over to Ol Banyan. When Monkey find he a hollow up there, he wrap he tail round heself cosy-cosy. An' quick-as-quick, he asleep. Just like that.

But the frogs them, they not sleepin. No sir. They gettin real disgusted.

"How 'bout a little shiver, Mister King, sir, just to let us know you listenin." Buffo talkin low-low now.

"Who you, anyways, tell a King how he should do?" Bull Frog roar out.

"Why Settler not sayin something, Momma?" Baby Frog peepin.

"Hush up, Baby, this no time for askin." An' he momma cuddle him close.

"Well, things gettin disappointin for sure," Pinky

grumble. "We want a Settler what settle things. That the whole idea."

"Say, Uncle. What the frogs them gon' do now?" Goat butt in.

"You meddlin with me story, Mister. Listen an' you gon' find out." Lizard get on with the tellin.

It them little tree frogs what fix it up. How you like that? Them little tree frogs!

They thinkin, "Maybe he gon' like a ol-time tune." So they all-together bust out loud in a chorus.

SET-TLER SET-TLER,
You the one now.
SET-TLER SET-TLER,
Start the fun now.
SET-TLER, SET-TLER,
That the way now.
SET-TLER, SET-TLER,
Save the day now.

Then them frogs start in dancin an' singin for all they worth. That a sight to see, Red-Eye. Something to remember. An' Lizard pause right there. Rememberin!

∽

But Ol Banyan him, he don't do nothin at-all at-all. Not a leaf tremble, no sir. Not a limb shake. Not a rustle, not a creak. Nothin! Uh-uh, that ol tree just stand there, still-as-still. Well, Red-Eye, I tellin you plain. Things not lookin too good for them frogs. No sir! But it Monkey, Monkey heself, gon' save the day.

All that singin an' dancin an' shakin an' such went an' wake him up. He listen a minute. An' right away he see what goin' on. "Aha," he say to heself. "I in business now. Those frogs them want a Settler. Well, they gon' get they-self a Settler. *Me!* No workin, no worries, plenty food. Livin like a King!" Monkey sure please with heself.

"I gon' give it a try now," he think. So he shout out, "Stop all that chatterin, you hear? Hush up you mouth, I say."

An' the frogs them stop so sudden you could a hear a sugar-bird feather drift down in the wind.

"Now! You listenin?" Monkey gettin goin' good here. "I hungry! How I gon' think hard when I hungry, eh?"

"He right, he right." The frogs them talkin all the self-same time.

"What you heart's desire, eh?"

"What you really like, Settler?"

"What you pleasure?"

"What you want, what you want?"

"How 'bout some sweet banana, Mister King, sir?"

"A juicy mango go down easy-easy."

An' such.

Ah well, the frogs them scatter ever-which-way. An' they feelin so glad.

"Oh my, Settler talkin at last," Pinky whistle. "Things gettin better now for sure."

Pretty soon the frogs them comin back with more-than-more. They carryin banana, coconut, an' mango, papaya, fig, an' grape, an' star apple, an' every sweet thing you could imagine.

When Monkey see the frogs bringin all them good things, he can't hardly wait. He call out, "Okay, okay. That plenty!"

An then he give 'em a *order*. Oh, the frogs them so glad to get a order from they Settler. They ready for anything.

"You frogs, you got to walk round this pond here. Three times goin east an' three times goin west. An' you got to say, 'Oh yes, oh yes, our Settler be the best!' No lookin up now, or the order be *cancel*. When you finish, I gon' settle things round here good an' proper."

So the frogs them start walkin an' recitin, while Monkey slip down, quick-as-quick, an' grab all them goodies. An' here where it happen, Red-Eye! There be Pinky, as usual, lookin back when he should a been lookin front. It Pinky, all right, catch a little peep a the tip-end a Monkey's tail.

"Something funny goin' on here," Pinky mutter. An' he search round hard for Blinky an' Buffo. "I seen somethin, an' I don't know what," Pinky say. "But look there, all the sweet things them gone. How that happen so fast, eh? Come on. We gon' find out."

An' them three frogs, they slip off in the bush. An' they sit there watchin, careful-careful.

Meanwhile, Monkey sittin up there in his takin-it-

easy spot, eatin banana an' drinkin coconut water. An' he happy.

"This be better than best," he laughin. "It too good to be true. I gon' play this game on the safe side. Make it last long-long."

So here come the rest a the frogs them. Back from they order an' gettin set to do some settlin. They testin out a little quarrelin on the way, just to see how it go.

"Hey, remember that ol mud hole, I say it mine, you say it yours?" Grichi sayin. "We gon' see who right, who wrong, soon-soon."

Oh, but it all in fun, you know. They in a good mood now. 'Cause they got a Settler, so things gon' settle.

"Mister King, sir," Bull Frog call out. "If you ready, we ready!" An' they all calm down quiet-quiet.

Okay. So here Monkey, comin in for the big time.

"I gon' show them frogs a thing or two," he say to heself. An' he shout out, "Moon shine, things fine."

"That don't mean nothin much," Monkey thinkin, "but it gon' sound good to all them, for sure."

Well, the frogs them start jabberin.

"What he say?"

"What that signify?"

"You hear that?"

An' such.

"Moon shine, things fine," Monkey shout again. An' he voice come out so loud he tail stand-up straight-straight.

An' it *Pinky* does see it. Yeah, he see it all right. He out in the bush there watchin, an' he see it!

"Look you," Pinky talkin soft now. "Way-up, way-up." An' he show where the tail stickin out the tree.

"Who that, who that?" Blinky want to know.

"I never see such a thing, up to now," Buffo snort. "The tree not talkin, *he* talkin."

"This a disgrace, all right. He makin believe he a Settler!" An' Pinky start gettin real fuss-up. "What kind a namby-pamby you call this? He not rulin us, he foolin us!"

"Hey, hey," Buffo call out. "You! What you doin up there?"

"I just passin through, Brother, just passin through," Monkey mumble.

"Don't you Brother me. I no brother to you." Pinky gettin steam-up all right.

"How come you sittin up there in our Settler, eh?" The three a them gettin real hot now.

"Uh-oh. Things not goin so good," Monkey say to heself. He start gettin worry.

Okay. So then the other frogs them hear the rumpus an' they come hoppin round to see what all goin' on.

Things movin pretty fast, all right. An' Pinky him, he jumpin all over the place.

"What you think a that?" he squealin. "A double-dealer, a two-face, a no-good ..." Pinky jumpin to beat the band. Well, when Monkey see they done catch him out, he know the game over.

"I better get goin' while the goin' good," he say, an' he start to climb.

I tell *you*, climbin be one thing Monkey do very very exceptional! So he climb an' he climb. Straight up-top a Big Ol Banyan. An' then he wrap he tail round a strong-strong limb. An' he swing. He swing right into that neighbour-tree. Bap! An' he there. See, if there be one thing Monkey do better than climbin, it swingin! So before them frogs know what happenin, there be Monkey ...swingin from tree to tree for all he worth. Headin for a five-star escape! An' sooner-than-soon he down by Grapetree Beach. Well, when Monkey see a piece a bamboo floatin out on the sea-water, he know he safe.

"That how I come, an' that how I gon' go," he say.

Uh-uh, he better look out. 'Cause the frogs them comin over the hill. An' they plenty mad, believe you me. But this the funny part, Red-Eye. Get this! They never did catch that Monkey, no sir. 'Cause he jump on the bamboo and he go with the tide! An' the frogs them...you

know frogs can't never take a drop a salty water on they skin. Not even a drop! So they just got to stand there, watchin. An' Monkey him, he way-away.

Goat look up an' cock he head to one side. "You mean …?" he start to ask.

"Exactly," Lizard answer. "An' the frogs them never get they Settler, neither. They still lookin."

"How 'bout Monkey?" Goat wonderin.

"Oh, Monkey," Lizard say. "He gone. He gone for good. Yes sir! From that day to this, you never gon' find no Monkey on this island. A monkey-no-climb tree, maybe. An' a monkey-puzzle sticky-bush, maybe. But Monkey heself, no sir!"

Then for a surprise, Lizard just bust right out with a ol-time tune.

How that Monkey come here
What that Monkey do
How that Monkey leave here
I been tellin you.
Goin 'cross the island
Every here an' where
Tree or bush may bear he name
But Monkey never there!

"I never knowed you could sing, Uncle," Goat blurt out.

"Live an' learn," Lizard chuckle. "Live an' learn. See Red-Eye. Now you can quit fussin 'bout *that* question, an' grab youself some sleep."

An' Lizard close he eyes. That what Lizards do, you know. 'Cause when they done, they done.

Keepin Secrets

*"Every story got to
have a threat!"*

Not every story a true story, me darlin. See, some story
happen…some story could a happen. But *this* story a *true*
story. I know, 'cause Grasshopper tell me the whole thing.
He there. An' he see it all.

Now, Grasshopper one a them frisky kind a creatures.
He here, he there, he all over the place. But it real hard
to see him out there in the grass. 'Cause he green like
grass…an' he long like grass…an' he move like grass…but
he not *grass*, no sir. He grasshopper! So. He get to see a
lot a secrets. But he don't tell 'em, uh-uh. He just keep
'em for later.

So one day he see Goat walkin along. Maybe he does
call it walkin, but not me. I call it scramblin. An' Goat,
he lookin round…see what he can get. Yeah, Goat curious, you know. An' he all-time hungry too. Okay. So that

when he see it, a small-small, all-over-dirty bunch a nothin much, just lyin there. But when Goat look close, he see it movin, just a little. And then he know it a livin thing.

"Poor baby," Goat say. "It all shiverin an' everything."

An' here where the idea come to him.

"I gon' take her home," he say.

Chile, it a wonder he ain' eat it when he see it. 'Cause Goat does eat most everything he see, *usual*. But this one time, he don't! Uh-uh, don't ask me why. There a mystery to things, sometimes.

So. He pick her up, gentle-gentle, an' he carry her home in his mouth. Can you *imagine*? All that way, he carry her…over to where the land drop down an' make a lovely valley. It take a time to reach, all right. But when they there, they there.

It one a them out-the-way places…quiet, peaceful, an' private-private. It all set about with hills for climbin. It have a tibit tree for shade, grass for eatin and a little freshwater spring near by. Yeah, it got everything he need. An' he on his own, too, the way he like it. See, it not that Goat unsociable or anything. No siree! It just that he *like* livin by himself. Well…he *did* like livin by himself till now…till Baby come on the scene.

"You gon' be happy here, Baby," Goat tell her. An' he put her down easy-easy. "That what I gon' call you," Goat decide. "I gon' call you Baby."

Oh yeah, Goat a smart fella, an' he know a lot. He see she smaller-than-small. An' she can't do nothin. So he figure, "She a baby, all right."

"I got to take good care a her," Goat thinkin. So he start gettin the place fix up. I *know*. Goats messy like anything, *usual*. But this goat got a kind a neatness 'bout his ways. He know how to make a place comfortable...cosy-cosy...so he do it.

"She got to be thirsty," Goat think. So he bring her some a that nice fresh water.

"Come on," he say. "Have a sip."

An' Baby take a sip.

So things improvin now. They settlin down.

Well, pretty soon, it evenin time. An' sudden-like, darkness come an' cover everything. Out there in the bush, croak answerin screech. Uh-huh, the night noises them startin up.

"I frighten," Baby whimper.

But Goat just give her a soft nuzzle an' say, "You don't need to frighten, honey. I here. I here." An' Goat lay himself down so, just 'side Baby. An' things better.

Well, day-by-day, time passin. Goat takin care a Baby fine-fine. He keepin a close watch on her. He bringin her good things for eatin...an' he tellin her joke...an' so on an' so on. See, he makin a home for Baby. An' he startin to *love* that little one. An' the love comin from Goat like a tree givin shade. It a natural-born love … an' that the best kind, you know. So, me darlin, you see how them two gettin on, eh? Baby growin. She gettin bigger. An' Goat him, he gettin happier. Every hour a the day an' night, Goat there … an' he doin things for Baby.

"You growin good," Goat say. "Baby, you *thrivin*." An' he please with heself.

A course, Grasshopper come by, every now and then, checkin on them. He just watchin … seein how it all workin out.

"I never knowed Goat lonely," he say to heself. "I bet *Goat* never knowed he lonely…till now he got company, an' he not *lonely* no more. Look there, he feelin different …an' he like it."

So. That the way it be, for a long-long time…them two, just livin in peace an' contentment. An' Grasshopper, he not tellin nobody nothin. So they secret safe.

Okay. So things goin' good, all right. But, a course, Baby changin all the while. A little here…a little there. Her feathers them start growin glossy, an' she stouten up, gettin plump, an' her wings comin out-out.

"What all *this*?" she wonderin.

Well, before you know it, she *beautiful*. Yeah, she a real beauty, all right.

Now, listen close sweetheart. 'Cause it a *secret* I gon' tell you. See, Baby a *bird*. What you think a that, eh? Yeah, she a *bird*. But she don't know it. 'Cause she never seen a bird beforetimes. An' when her talkin change from peep to warble…well, she wonderin 'bout that too…but she don't *know*.

"Why I got two feet an' Billy got four?" she thinkin. (She does call him Billy for fun.) "An' he got whiskers hangin down-side his chin. An' he got horns up-top his head, too." That what she askin herself. But she so happy with Goat…well… she not wonderin too much.

An' Goat, he so busy teachin Baby goat-ways to do things, he not noticin all them changes. Chile, *everybody* know you can't never turn a bird into a goat, never! But Goat forget all 'bout that. Maybe, a long time back, he knowed it. But he forget it now. 'Cause his heart full a love for Baby, an' he want her to stay, so he keep on teachin.

An' Baby, she good at learnin. Every day she gettin better an' better. She reachin higher... she huntin in the bush... she pullin grass... she scramblin on them rocks. Yeah, she learnin!

So. It come about one mornin, Goat up before day. An' it lovely... cool-cool.

"Say," Goat think. "I goin' down to East End... search out a special treat for Baby." An' while Baby sleepin quiet-quiet, all snug under Good Ol Tibit, he slip away.

Uh-*uh!* This the time Goat go an' get careless. He forget how far it be to East End. An' he forget how long it take, gettin back. So Baby on her own, eh?

Anyway, faster-than-fast, Goat gone down East, an' he huntin somethin unusual, somethin Baby gon' love.

An' back in the valley, that little one stirrin. She up. She up an' out... lookin round... seein what's what.

"Ooh," Baby whisper. "*There* somethin."

See, she spy a shiny-shiny red-red somethin poppin

out up-top a sticky-bush. That where she see it. It a *berry* … a fat red berry … a fat red *juicy* berry. An' Baby want it.

Now. Goat all-time get them high-up things. He snatch 'em off easy, an' he bring 'em down quick, an' he give 'em to Baby. But look. Goat not there, no. An' Baby gon' try it on her own.

Oh me darlin, this the part I can't hardly tell! Baby reachin, but she can't reach high-up so. She try. She try climbin an' scramblin an' shakin the branches them. She try every-each goat-way she know. She try gettin to that berry. An' she can't!

Well. Baby vex, all right. She so vex, she jumpin up an' down. An'... in the middle a all that jumpin ... she just sort a *stay up*! How that happen, eh? See, what it is ... she take a little fly-up, just by accident. She don't know she doin it, 'cause she never done it before. Ah, but she doin it now, all right.

So. She *fly* here, *fly* there. Just tryin it out, see. An' she lovin it. She real tickle with this new way a gettin round.

"This what-you-call-it great," she screech. She *that* tickle.

So meanwhile Goat down at East End, huntin an' scratchin an' pullin an' diggin. He busy, all right. But when he look up an' see the sun so high-high ... he *know* he gone too long. Uh-*huh*! So he make for home fast. Goat nimble, you know. His feet dainty-dainty. But they sure-footed too. An' when he movin, he movin! Yeah, there he go ... cuttin through the bush like a beetle through a field full a 'cane.

But when he reach home ... oh, he surprise, in truth. First thing he see is Baby, flyin all over the place.

"What you think you doin?" Goat shout. "You makin a spectacle a youself." An' he shake his horns an' he stamp his feet.

"Rest youself, Billy. Rest youself." Baby laughin now.

Goat standin by a red-belly tree, so she settle down on it, nice-as-nice. "Say! This fun. This *real* fun. You got to try it sometime."

See, me darlin, Baby still don't *know*. She think Goat can do it too. Oh yeah, she delighted, all right. An' the flyin comin easy-easy now.

"Why you makin so much fuss, Billy?" she ask him. Baby swoopin round Goat's head ... she showin off.

"Baby, you not talkin sensible," Goat bawl out.

Oh, he actin vex, for true. But see, he more *sad* than vex. 'Cause he know things changin. Yeah, the ol times them gone for good.

"This great," Baby screech.

But Goat know it *not* great. "This got to be me bad-luck day," he mumble. "Why I go an' stay so long from Baby? That when all this mess-up start."

Well. Now Baby learn to do *this*, who know what comin next. When things change, they change. An' they's no goin back, neither.

So. Time passin, an' Baby enjoyin this flyin stuff like anything. She gettin them high-up berries, an' she practicin stop-an'-go, an' she cleanin her feathers them. She learnin, all right.

"Hey, Billy! Things sure different from up here," she call out. Baby sittin up-top that red-belly. She lookin high an' low. An' she happy.

Uh-huh, Baby growin up now. She explorin the place like crazy. An' that day got to come when she fly up, way up, higher-than-*high* up. Yeah, she lookin for cloud, tell if rain comin or no. An' then Baby see somethin' far-far off ...somethin' she never see beforetimes. Goat gone. He out in the bush, huntin things as usual. So she alone...an' she frighten.

See, me darlin, Baby one a them two-by-two birds. Pelicans, everybody does call 'em. Pelicans! But they *two-by-two birds*, all right. An' if you see one, sure-as-sure you gon' see another. An' here come that other, flyin over Blue Mountain...flyin high an' comin straight for *there*.

So. The closer he come, the more Baby see. An' soon, she not frighten no more. Chile, she *glad*. She so glad to see that other. You can't be*lieve* how glad she be. She seein somethin' just like she...brown, ruffle-up feathers ...wings bigger-than-big...scaly-scale feet (two a them)... everything same-same.

An' when that other bird come to settle down quiet on Ol Tibit, Baby get her courage back.

"What your name?" she ask.

"Pelican," he tell her. "*Big* Pelican," he say. And he stretch his wings way-out...an' he shake 'em.

"My, my." Baby lookin at him. "I like when you do that."

"Oh, that nothin." Big Pelican all embarrass. "I got lots a other tricks better'n that." An' he smilin now.

"Where you from?" Baby ask him.

"A place over to Salt Pond," he say. "A couple of coconut palms by the water. Things real sociable there. Lots a birds an' all." *That* what Big Pelican tell her.

"Say! What a *bird?*" Baby ask him.

"What a *bird?*" Big Pelican can't believe she ask him *that.* "Honey, *you* a bird," he tell her. "You not *know* that? Whoo-eee!" An' he flyin all round an' he laughin like anything.

Well, me darlin, things movin fast now. Baby know she a *bird,* an' she merry. She flyin high, all right. An' all them goat-ways a thing a the past.

"What *your* name?" Big Pelican ask her.

"Baby," she tell him.

"Well, Baby," he say. "I gon' show you a lot a things." An' he puff himself up... an' he beat the air with his wings in a mighty rush.

So. That how it all start out. In them afternoons, when the sun hidin his face back a Ol Tibit, an' Goat off huntin things in the bush. *That* when they start this gettin-together. It not that Baby keepin Big Pelican secret from Billy, no sir! It just that she sort a two-minded 'bout it. An' while she thinkin it out, she ain't sayin nothin.

Grasshopper in on it, a course. He out there in the grass...an' he not givin no sign that he there. But he there.

"Well, well," he chuckle, "so that how things shapin up, eh? Uh-uh. Pretty soon, somethin got to give." An' then, quick as a flash, he gone. That Grasshopper!

So, Baby an' Big Pelican meetin. They flyin an' talkin, talkin an' flyin. An' Baby learnin things she never know before. She hearin 'bout other birds an' they ways an' they places an' such.

"You got to *see* it, Baby," Big Pelican sayin. "It not like here at-all. It *different*."

An' Baby listenin. An' one a them days, she get an idea. It a hazy *after*noon, one a them lazy-dazy, do-nothin *after*noons, when she come out with it.

"Take me down to Salt Pond," she tell Big Pelican. Well! It hot, *real* hot. An' he drowsin on a limb a Red-Belly. An' he don't feel like movin.

"Ah, come on, Baby. It too hot for hot," he say.

But you know Baby. When she get a notion, she gon' move on it.

"No, no. I want to *see* the place," she say. "You all-time tellin me it *this*, it *that*. Well, I ready to have a look."

So, Big Pelican can't do nothin but carry her there.

Meanwhile, down in the valley, Goat on his way. He

bringin a tasty treat for Baby, an' he rushin. But when he reach home, it awful quiet ... too quiet. So Goat start lookin round.

See, beforetimes Goat never raise up his voice to Baby. He all-time gentle with her, you know. But now he raise it up, all right ... he that *worry*.

"Baby," he bawl out. "Where you hidin? You playin trick? You foolin with me, eh? Come on, Baby. Come *on*."

But Baby not comin, me darlin. An' soon, Goat know it for *real*. Baby gone! See, it seem that Goat never seen Big Pelican at-all. An' he never hear 'bout the other birds them down by Salt Pond, an' all that. So. He don't know. Well, he just sit down under that good-ol' tibit tree, an' he puzzle ... an' he puzzle ... but he can't puzzle it out, nohow.

"What happen?" he thinkin. "Where Baby now?"

Let me tell *you*, that a hard day for Goat.

"The good times done pass me by," he mutter. "How I come to find me Baby gone? I knowed that flyin business was bad business," Goat frettin. "Now she went an' fly so high, she don't know how to get back down. Poor Baby." An' he worryin himelf to pieces.

Well. Grasshopper, he out there in the grass and he don't know what it is he got to do. *He* know 'bout Big Pelican. He seen the two a them talkin an' flyin round the

place. But Grasshopper, he not a interferer…an' he never been one. So he don't say nothin! He just sit there, quiet. An' he wait.

Now. This the part I like to tell. 'Cause believe me, I know you feelin sorry for Goat. You so tender-hearted, me darlin. Well. Just 'bout mid-ways 'tween sun-high-up an' sun-goin-down … that when it happen. First, it just a black speck a nothin, way up off to the west… an' Goat not seein it. He still puzzlin an' ponderin… an' gettin nowheres. Uh-uh, an' that black speck gettin bigger. An' soon it look like it not *just* a black speck, it a *lot* a black specks…big ones, small ones, movin along pretty good… comin closer all the while. An' what you think it is, eh? Aha, you right! It *Baby*, comin home. But she not on her own, uh-*uh*. She bringin company!

You think Goat happy or *what*? Yeah, he happy all right. He see his Baby. An' he see the others them too. But he see his Baby. So he not worryin no more.

"Hey, Billy," Baby callin to him. She flyin lower now …gettin ready to touch down. "I bringin us some company," she sing out. Well, maybe Baby not much of a singer, but she tryin anyhow.

An' pretty soon they all there. Baby, Big Pelican, an' a bunch a them others… a couple a frigates, a couple a boobies, some sparrows, some doves, an' even a yellow-breast or two.

"What all *this?*" Goat askin in wonderment.

"See." Baby smilin now. "Big Pelican a friend a mine. He the one tell me 'bout Salt Pond an' all. It real *sociable* down by Salt Pond, Billy. But it gettin a little *too* sociable, sort a push-an'-mash, if you know what I mean. So they lookin for a new place…a quiet, peaceful, private-private place. That when I tell them 'bout *our* place."

An' then Baby tell him, soft-soft, "I a *bird*, you know, Billy. An' the others them, *they* birds too."

Well, Goat don't know *what* to say. He never before see so *many* birds all bunch-up together. They singin, they chatterin, they twitterin. They lookin here an' there. They lively all right! An' they satisfy, too.

"What you think?" Big Pelican askin them others. "Just what I tell you, eh?" He please with himself.

Yeah, all the birds them settlin in, makin things homey. An' Baby, she prouder-than-proud.

But look. There Grasshopper, out in the bush. An' he laughin. "Well, well. Goat never gon' be lonely no more," he say. "All them birds, they gon' keep him busy now for sure. Ain't it a *shame* I can't never tell this story to *nobody*. 'Cause who ever gon' believe it, eh?"

But one day Grasshopper tell it to me, me darlin, an' now I tellin it to you. Yeah, Goat, he all-time busy with the birds them and they babies. An' when he stop an' look round his secret valley, it *sure* different.

"Ah well," Goat say to himself. "The more the merrier." An' he shake his whiskers … an' he wrinkle his nose … an' he off … huntin treats, *as usual*.